Sebastian...

The Incredible Drawing Dog

THE MAN WHO MADE CUSTARD

Story and pictures by DAVID MYERS
from the television series devised and written by David Myers

MB MARILYN MALIN BOOKS
in association with ANDRE DEUTSCH

For Joy, Jane, Paul,
Adam and Matthew

First published 1987 by Marilyn Malin Books
in association with André Deutsch Ltd
105-106 Great Russell Street, London WC1B 3LJ

Text and illustrations copyright © 1987 David Myers

British Library Cataloguing in Publication Data

Myers, David
   The man who made custard. – (Sebastian the
   incredible drawing dog/David Myers)
   I. Title   II. Series
   823'.914 [J]   PZ7
   ISBN 0-233-98067-9

Hello, dear reader,

What a strange title for a book, isn't it?   Well, to be truthful it's a VERY strange tale.

I had a splendid time doing the pictures and I do hope you will like them.   Poor Mr. O'Duffy has SO many problems.   Don't worry though because all ends well.   But promise not to look at the last pages yet!

Now I must get on with my next book.

See you soon!

With best wishes,

Sebastian...

PS. I rather like custard, but frankly, I hate the skin on top.......

Archibald O'Duffy was a small man to look at, but his ambition was *great*!! GREAT!! Let me tell you about it....

Whereas many people wish to become doctors, lawyers, scientists, engineers, chemists, etc., Archibald O'Duffy wanted only ONE thing in life.

You will hardly believe this but it is *true*! Do you know what his burning ambition was? He wanted to own a *custard* factory!

A CUSTARD factory!! The FINEST custard factory there ever was!! Fame and fortune would be his! His name would go down in history!

Unfortunately he possessed little money...

but by chance, close to his home there stood a very
old and delapidated warehouse. The roof was leaky,
the brick walls crumbling and the floors full of cracks.

But, because of its dreadful condition Mr O'Duffy was able to buy it at a low price. This is how the warehouse looked. Pretty grim, don't you agree? Look at the shocking state of it.

Nevertheless, with tremendous flair and energy
Mr O'Duffy set about making the place ship-shape.

Unable to afford help of any kind, he did all the building work himself. Bricklaying, cementing, sawing,

painting – you name it – he did it.

It was a mammoth struggle but within six
weeks, four days and seven hours it was complete.

Next he installed huge tubs in which to store his cooking
materials, giant vats in which to mix the ingredients

and a vast mechanical spoon to stir and stir and stir....

But then, oh dear, then his troubles began. No matter how he tried, the end result was always the same! His custard tasted *awful*!! AWFUL!!

"Whatever am I to do?" he moaned. "No self-respecting shopkeepers are going to buy it. They'd lose all their customers in no time! *No* time at all! What am I to do?"

Every single day he would attempt a new recipe. A splash of this – a dash of that. A grain of this – a sprinkling of that. But to no avail. It always tasted DREADFUL!

Just look at his face as he tested a spoonful!

Each time he would spit it out in disgust, rush to the sink and wash out his mouth with gallons of water.

How many people can you see in my picture?

Mr O'Duffy was distraught! So terribly distraught that he flung on his coat and hat…

and rushed off to a fortune-teller, Madame Zola, who
lived near by.

Isn't it a strange room?

Here she is seated at her table.

will he? won't he?

As she gazed into her crystal ball, he looked up at her and cried, "Please, Madame Zola, *please* tell me – am I ever going to succeed in my life's work? Will my dream *ever* come true?"

Madame Zola stared into the crystal ball. For minutes she remained silent. Then she spoke.

"Mr O'Duffy, the crystal tells all! The crystal does not lie!

Heavens – let's hope the good news is really good!!

"First I will give you the *bad* news – you will *never*, NEVER make a good custard! You will always make a THICK, DISGUSTING, VILE, FOUL-TASTING custard!!"

Poor Mr O'Duffy was shattered! SHATTERED! Taking
out a large red handkerchief, he began to sob bitterly.

"Mr O'Duffy," cried Madam Zola, "listen, listen to me!
You haven't heard the *good* news yet!" Once more she
stared into the crystal ball....

"The good news is – the *GOOD* news is – your THICK, DISGUSTING, VILE, FOUL-TASTING custard is going to bring you *fame* and *fortune*!! I can tell you no more, but untold riches will be yours and your name will go down in history!!"

Mr O'Duffy was overjoyed! Thanking Madam Zola
for putting his mind at rest, he raced back to the factory.
   Here he goes, head erect, whistling a merry tune and
chuckling with glee.

Can you guess who is ringing?...

No sooner had he reached the factory than the telephone rang.

Things are looking up!!

Lifting the receiver, he said, "O'Duffy's custard at your service!!"

A voice at the other end shouted, "Can you supply me with 50,000 gallons of your custard. NO, NO, I've changed my mind – make it 100,000 gallons. I'll send round our fleet of tanker lorries tomorrow to collect!" Then the line went dead.

And so it came about. That very next morning, twenty
huge tankers arrived at the factory. By lunch time they
were all loaded with Mr O'Duffy's THICK,
DISGUSTING, VILE, FOUL-TASTING custard.
And then they were off! With engines roaring they
rumbled away from the factory....

What a success story!

Well, true to Madam Zola's words, Mr Archibald O'Duffy made his fortune. He now lives in a palatial mansion surrounded by acres and acres of fabulous garden. And what's more – every single drop of his custard is bought by the same customer.

In fact if you go to any city, town, village or hamlet, you can see the result of Mr O'Duffy's astounding success.

Cheerio for now!!

Just look at the roads in all the NO PARKING areas.
There you will see those endless thick, yellow lines.
Miles and miles and miles of them.

Most people believe they are made of yellow paint.
But you and I know quite differently. Don't we?